A Bold Walk to Happiness

Brett Miller

A Bold Walk to Happiness

tellwell

Tellwell Talent
www.tellwell.ca

ISBN
978-0-2288-8142-1 (Hardcover)
978-0-2288-8141-4 (Paperback)
978-0-2288-8143-8 (eBook)

What makes you happy in the grand picture of things is a pretty broad question, if you ask me. The thing we have to look at is what will make us happy. I tell you happiness is not going to be in something or even people per say but rather in being truly happy with yourself to go out there in the universe and kick ass. Also, you can show your love to others because you have a love for yourself within.

Let me tell you a story. When I was twenty-five years old, I was going home from my parents' house, driving my car, and I was getting severe chest pains. The more I drove, the worse it got. I walked into my house, where some renters lived with me. Also, my sister lived with me. When I walked in the door, the pain worsened. I went upstairs, returned ten minutes later, and collapsed on the living room floor. I immediately got dizzy and had severe pain because I couldn't breathe. My sister came down the stairs and called 911. The ambulance showed up, and when I made it to the hospital, I couldn't comprehend how I got there. Nurses came in and hooked me up too many things, and then in walked my buddy's ex-girlfriend. I'm like, *Here we go, the nurse who likes to steal napkins from the Dairy Queen; what a class act.* At this time, she stabbed some needles in me, laughing the whole time. I also had an IV bag hooked up. The pain kept getting worse, and by now I was passed out. When I woke up, the lights were out.

The doctor came in, and he said, "Good morning, Mr. Miller. The good news is you're not dead. The bad news is you have a blood clot that started in your right leg that was fourteen inches long. Half of it broke off into both of your lungs, and the other half went into your heart. You just had a stroke, and I'm not sure how you're still sitting here breathing. We will try our best to keep you going, but I can't guarantee."

My priest came in to pray for me as the days went by. I remember we were talking about the love of Jesus and how we can conquer all by what he put in us. At that moment, I knew Jesus. Still, I didn't know God at this type of hour. Having a doctor tell you "I'm glad you're not dead" was an absolute miracle in my eyes and made me realize how life is pretty short. I asked myself what I wanted to do with my life because what I was currently doing was not fulfilling. *Am I going to keep on doing the same old stuff, or am I going to explore my options and set out to find what I want to do with my life?* Let me ask you this: When you go to sleep at night, are you fulfilled? And hey! You may make great money, but are you happy to the core? When we look at true happiness, we have to be satisfied with ourselves, but if you're doing something right now that you hate or just like, how will that work for you long term? We live in this "kind-of-like" society. *I like this person, but I don't get fired up to be with them. I like this job, but I don't go jumping out of bed to go after it and light it up. I want to get married someday to this person, but I won't be upset if it does not happen. I like this business adventure, but I will not get too frustrated if it doesn't work out.* When we look at our goal, dream, gift, and what we were born to do, we can't have a Plan B because Plan B is a waste of time. It would be best to only have a Plan A. *I will do this come hell or high water; this is what God has put inside me to do. I will get the job done no matter what, and no one will separate God and me for what he has planned for my life.* It's hard for me not to laugh when I see people always running to people to give them an answer. Let me ask you this about me, someone with sin and flaws. How do you expect me to provide you with something that God can give you? I hate to tell you it will never happen.

What amazed me was how little I knew and how weak my vocabulary was when I first started reading the Bible. When we think of things that can create unhappiness, some examples come to mind. Social media will plant this seed inside of you; if you spend too much time with it, you will become obsessed with comparing your life to someone else's. You will be looking at their stuff and going, *Wow, my life doesn't look as good as theirs. How can I expect these thoughts of happiness long term when I'm constantly comparing my life to someone else's?* Understand that your life is unique to you and that God gave us all a unique life at birth.

Another thing that comes to mind is lust and pornography. Pornography will give you this sense to only look at a person's physical appearance and body and what it could do for you. By basing the relationship on sex, when we look at someone lustfully, rather than getting to know the person, we may find out that this person who has the desirable physical appearance does not have the attitude or personality we were looking for. Here are some helpful tips for modern ladies: if you want a committed relationship with a man, start by getting to know the man before having sex with him. See if he has willpower and see if he likes you as a person and not just based on what you can do for him sexually. Understand this, though: unless the man likes dudes or is very deep-rooted in his religion and committed to celibacy before marriage, he will never say no. If you remove all your clothes for a man and expect him to have the willpower to say no, guess what? It will never happen. He's not going to say, "Oh, don't worry about it. I will catch you next time." Men, in general, aren't programmed like this. Also, a man can have sex with a woman and feel absolutely nothing after. Just because he has sex with you doesn't mean he will want a relationship after the fact. If I see a woman willing to let it all loose for next to nothing, I don't look at her as relationship material. It's like this: *You're showing me you don't respect yourself enough to let me fight for you, so how do I expect you to show me any respect in a relationship? And how do I expect you to say you could love me when you're willing to give it up for next to nothing?*

There is a difference between having sex and making love. Sex will always be driven by having this "kind of" attitude at the back of your mind: *Let's try this relationship out. If it does not work, no sweat; I'm not going to be to upset.* Making love with a person is different; you feel a deep-rooted connection with this person, and you give a shit about the outcome, and you will be upset and hurt if things don't work out. I'm looking for a woman who likes who she is, who is a bit of a rebel, and who isn't always going to tell me good news. Why, you might ask? Because I want a challenge. I get bored very quickly. For the most part, I would say that men don't care what a woman does for a living or how much money she makes. We are happy to date a girl who works at the corner store. In the grand picture of things, what a woman does for a living is not a priority. Men don't care about labels, but if you are a career woman, understand you are making a sacrifice if you decide to do so. Hey, there's nothing wrong with that.

Here's a funny story: I remember back when I was going to high school, I was very intrigued with this one woman, and from a physical standpoint, she was not a girl you would go, "Oh wow, she is a knockout. Her physical beauty is radiating." No, not at all, but what I found about her when we all hung out in a group was her level of intelligence. She was super intuitive and knew what she wanted and where she was going. Her ability to convey and project with absolute certainty that she knew what she was doing and had her goals written down and how she wanted to accomplish them I found to be a huge turn on. For myself, over the years, as I have grown as a person and advanced to a new level and new heights, I have always tried to hang around more intelligent people than me because I realize if I keep doing this, the more my thinking is going to expand and the more of an impact I'm going to make not only on my life but also on the lives of others.

Recently, over the last few years, I have become good friends with a priest. I started going to a different church because I moved, and at the end of the day, I'm glad I did. He has become a mentor to me and is a book of knowledge when I talk to him. It's hard to fathom, but I was raised Catholic and brought up in the church, and until I started going to his church, I had not experienced the gospel quite like that since I was a bean sprout, growing up in Ontario, Canada. It's not really a common thing when you're a thirty-year-old man to say to someone, "Yah, I go to church every Sunday." Church is almost like a foreign thing to most people. For myself, if I were to give my two cents, Millennials and Gen Z, for the majority, are constantly into so many different things. The number of other things I've heard people are into is astronomical. It's an endless supply. For myself, when I go to church, I am very engaged and get a lot out of the sermon not only because I am very into it, but also because of the amount of energy and confidence my priest exudes when he is up in the pulpit. Like anything in life, people follow strength. Strength usually comes with a certain amount of authority, like when Jesus got mad the one time and turned the table of the money changers (the people who were committing wrongful acts). When I get up to speak in the pulpit as a lector, or when I am speaking anywhere else, I speak with authority. Why? Because people listen more closely to what you're saying when there is depth and character in your voice and you're not there to mess around and keep it boring. Ask yourself this: How long would you say your attention span is, for the most part? Would you say you are someone who can listen for hours on end about something, or would you say your attention almost comes in spurts, to a certain degree? By being engaged in anything, there is going to have to be a level of wanting to know more. There needs to be a bit of mystery. The way you articulate and project your speech will determine how you are perceived and how people react to you. I'm going to tell you this: Not everyone will be on board and believe what you're saying, and that's ok, because not everyone will be for you. If I had a dollar for every time I thought someone would be supportive, I would be a multimillionaire by now, but believing in yourself to an unstoppable degree requires looking at something besides yourself and in the form of a higher power. In my opinion, the gospel is the most motivational book ever written. There are so many underlying stories that can relate to something going on with your own life right here and right now.

I found when I first started reading the Bible how poor and how intrinsic, rationalized, and common my grammar was. For the vast majority of people I encounter, what I was projecting in my speech wasn't too methodical; it was just something that was stagnant. You could say I was not getting to the ulterior motive. I was just basically saying stuff for the gratification of pleasing people, and over time, that is never a good thing. Don't be afraid of ruffling some feathers and standing up when it is necessary to do. I'm at the point in my life where I seek to do what's right, and if it means breaking some rules, then so be it. I would rather do the right thing and ask for forgiveness later than do the wrong thing and keep living not in the truth in a life that doesn't align with my beliefs.

When you first step out and decide to bet on yourself, and always had the right stuff, it will be scary. I've always been an underdog type of person. I never had anyone ever tell me "You're so exceptional." Things I love to do have always been work for me. Funny story: I remember when I was going to elementary school, Our Lady of Fatima it was called, and they dragged me into a room the one day. This was about Grade Three. They were like, "Well, Mr. Miller, since you don't learn like the rest of the students, we are going to put you on this individual education plan." This was another way of secretly telling me that I was stupid. I saw that on my report card all the way up till I graduated high school. It caused me great anger and frustration. I felt like, *You don't know me for shit, and how dare you try to give your opinion of me, because guess what? It's not going to become my reality. I deserve better than that.* I believe the education system has failed a lot of people. In life and with how things are structured, there are no guarantees. I know dozens of people who are way more educated than me, yet at the end of the day, they have no better job than me. How does that make sense at the end of the day if you always rely on people to give you this amazing answer to the extent that "If you do this, you will have it all figured out"? Life doesn't work like that. It is full of ups and downs with wins and losses, and the losses will usually far exceed the wins.

The thing about happiness is that it's all about progress. If we are all each and every day progressing to achieve one of our goals, then negative notions usually take the back seat. Learn to be mission-driven. *What will this mean if I do this?* and also *What will this mean in the lives of others if I fully dive into what I have been called to do?* Because it's about the calling. You can feel something in your heart if it directly aligns with who you are and your being of existence. There is no force on this entire Earth that will stop it if you are fully committed. Recognize who is for you and who is against you. I have done so many nice things for people who could not care at the end of the day what I do or who I am. It's fascinating how the human brain works, especially at this point in time. It's fascinating how far we have come as a society. A lot of things have become superficial and are based on looking for a glandular reward or a feeling from something or a mindset of *I'm deserving*. It's like the world does not owe me anything: I am the author and finisher of my story. Life is what you make it, who you choose to surround yourself with, and the energy you attract into your life. Doing what's right can be peaceful but also scary at the same time because you never know what the outcome will be until it happens. Let me ask you this: Does God want you to do what's right or wrong? Telling the truth and being real will get you to new heights and greater expansion, and hey, it might cost you something. Still, you will know. You will not be pondering a question, wondering "What if?" Life is way too short to ask "What if?" If you get shunned in the process, then so be it. Understand that not everyone will like you and like what you have to offer. People frown on stuff they don't have. I'm at a point where I am mission-driven. What do I want to accomplish? How will I do it? What is this gift God has put inside of me to fulfill? I GET LOST when I get writing and when I do other things like public speaking. When I'm in the zone, you could say I literally could go for hours as I write and write; I look at this book as a study guide. Read it and apply some steps you can take to your own life. I look at this book as a tool because multiple people have coached me and coaching costs. Coaching is not a cheap hobby, so how do I take some great ideas that I have learned in my own life to apply them to a book someone can afford and be able to keep with them? That's a win. Not only can I give back, but I can share a piece of me. I have taken the time and energy to write from the heart.

As we go through life, various things will bring us down. But how do we react to our emotions in the current moment? Do we focus on the good or the bad? Everything that goes up must come down in the rollercoaster of life. Ask yourself this personal question: When you wake up till the time you go to bed, on average, how many different emotions would you say you experience daily? I'm sure it's more than one. Ask yourself what you are allowing yourself to tolerate daily. Is your brain progressing into joyful harmonious thoughts, or is it keeping you stagnant and frustrated? When I think about emotions flowing freely, I think about my surroundings and the energy I let surround me. This can be compared to hanging around someone who mistreats you and won't go out of their way to do anything. In contrast, someone kind to you would give you the shirt off their back and exchange meaningful conversation. Which one do you think could lead to long-term results? The choice is pretty obvious. This would be like me going, "Well, I'm not too fond of the response I'm getting to what I'm writing, so I'm going to give up and try something else." Without commitment, nothing significant ever happens. I could quit and try something else, but guess what? The problem is still there when I leave, and it follows me. Without changing my mind first, the same old habits and patterns will follow me wherever I go. The old saying goes, "You can buy a new car, but if you put the old man in the new car, you'll still have the old experience." A life led by love is the recipe for a win or a future win. When we weren't given something when we were young, it's sometimes hard to justify when it happens years down the road. We think, *This is too good to be true; something is bound to mess up*, but I guess we are all human. Something is bound to happen. We all make mistakes, and we all mess up from time to time. Embrace it, and don't be so hard on yourself all the time. I have always battled this over the years because I'm very hard on myself to reach my goals. After all, it's all up to me, no one else. This book isn't going to write itself. I take responsibility that it's on me and only me. If I don't get what I want out of this book and express myself in a way that is readable and presentable, then that's totally on me.

Understand the need to take action and then some more action. Set up the right pieces to win, because guess what? Even though it's your responsibility to make it happen, you must also understand that you can't do it all alone. Surround yourself with people you can learn from, and work with people who are better at something than you. If I want good insights from the Bible, I go to my priest and he can break down exactly what it means to the very last word because he has mastered his calling. At the end of the day, he is a man of God. I could tell you stories that I know from the Bible, but when he tells it, it's on a whole other level, and by the time he is done his sermon, I always get something out of it. I usually go, "Jeez, I never thought about it like that." Because once you have mastered something, there are no limits to what you can accomplish. The possibilities are endless and unstoppable, because when you're in that type of zone where you are the author and the finisher by what you do and know the absolute ins and outs, it will affect everything in your life in a positive way. You are reaching and stretching to something newer and greater, something out of this world. When people look at you, they will say, "Jeez, that person made that look effortless and easy," but this all starts with commitment, because without commitment, nothing ever happens. How do you expect to be great at something and have it reflected in your bank account when you always have one foot in the door and one foot out? Life doesn't work like that for top performers. In every industry, the ones who are committed and who have the strongest work ethic always rise to the top in anything. I know people with the most random jobs who out-earn people with prestigious jobs, you could say, based on a worldview perspective. *I will, I must, I can be* is the attitude you must attain to rise to the top. When you get tired, keep going, because we will all be tired for good one day, and we don't know when that's coming. We all have one life to live, so why not live it to the fullest and make it the absolute best and create what we want to create? Make a difference in someone else's life and touch their heart by what you do. The effort will play a big part in the lives of all of us.

Are you putting effort into things you want to accomplish? That has always been the big thing for me. I can feel the lack of energy right away when I'm not into it. When we look at everything as a whole, like why I am upset right now, and especially how this whole pandemic has changed things and people's perspectives, it's all about division: getting people fired up on each side so they can divide people and turn them against one another. The devil's best thing is to isolate people, make them feel like they're no good, and turn them against one another over a matter of opinion. What were we all doing before all this unfolded? Can you think of a time when you thought things would be closed because of certain rules, especially here in Canada? That shouldn't deter you from doing something great in your life right here and now. You still have a lot to give as long as you breathe. Personally, when I have been down and not felt well, it's related to who I have been surrounding myself with to a certain extent. Your surroundings play into your thoughts and frame of mind big time. By hanging around a bunch of miserable people, sooner or later that will rub off and you too will start to feel miserable. Jim Rohn said it best when he said you're the total of the five people you most hang out with. This concept relates to an animal-type instinct of wanting to fit in with the pack and be part of the gang. People will sacrifice for what they truly believe in and bite their tongue to remain in the pack, even though they might disagree, because everyone wants to fit in to a certain extent.

As I have gotten older, I have made it a point to speak the truth, and if people don't like it, then so be it. I can't please everyone. Sometimes people ask me, "Why are you so aggressive?" I'm a man with testosterone running up and down my body. It's an instinct not to back down and fight for what I believe in. If you look at how young men and women are today compared to fifty years ago, so many things have changed. I truly believe that if you want to start living life to the fullest then form a relationship with God, there will be no greater force when you are down, than having God by your side and knowing what he has in store for you. People have sins. People have flaws. We all do, but with God, there is no mistake; there will be no greater feeling when you feel that energy rush into your heart. This feeling will be like no other. As I always say, "When a man turns a certain age, it's time to leave boy stuff behind." It's amazing how I run into people I have known for ten years, and they're doing the same shit. It's like, "No, bro, I haven't done any of that shit in years. My life over the last so many years has been self-development." How do I become the best version of myself I can be to become the hero of my own story? What are the things I tell myself? How do people view me when they first approach me? People lead by strength. The most you can do is attack every day like it's your last. How do I put myself in a position to win? Let me ask you this: How do you truly expect to win if you don't eat, breathe, and dive depths into the core of what you were created to do? Adapting to a high level will affect your life in every area to an inclination of abundant thoughts and unstoppable results.

Other things can also lead to unhappiness, such as drugs, alcohol, or whatever your vice is. Ask yourself this:

If you are currently doing whatever you frequently do, do you feel good the next day? Do you feel a seed of happiness waking up, or do you feel a seed of depressive thoughts coming in, like *Why did I do that? I feel like shit now; my head is pounding,* or *My stomach feels ready to explode.* Honestly, do you think doing this daily will benefit you long term and give you this everlasting fire of going out to tackle the day? So frequently nowadays you see people lost in space somewhere while they are at work. Ask yourself this, for whatever it may be for you: Do you like yourself when you're sober? Or do you simply put on a mask every day and have something take you to a state of mind, that for a short period, gives you a sense of peace and takes you away from all the things going wrong with your life? Here is the thing: the devil works overtime in everything he does. He will meet us in the parking lot and at the dinner party. There is no time or place he will not stop trying to take control of our thoughts so he can keep us not moving forward, and not pursuing what God intended for our life.

Over time, as I have come to understand, not everyone is a follower. Hey, I don't judge anyone, because if I do, I too shall be judged. Some people believe in the air, in the trees, in a variety of different types of energy, and the list goes on. I like to hear from every category as long as it promotes love at the end of the day. I've never been the type of person to be closed off; I'm always open to hear something from someone else. When you look at any romantic relationship, understand that looks fade. Someday we will all wake up, and we won't be as pretty as we once were. We will have to rely more on a loving personality to get us through the rough days because our partner won't be so pretty anymore from a physical standpoint. When you form any relationship with anyone, ask yourself if you love this person's personality. Could you see yourself spending days on end with them? If you have to ponder that question, you might want to reconsider rather than look at the material things or physical attributes this person might have to offer or the benefits they might have in their package. Learn to separate ego from spirituality, because if you drive the relationship based on ego, what will other people think when you're with that person in a relationship? Eventually, something will fail down the line, and it will not be subtle. It's going to be a blow-up-in-your face thing. When you're in a relationship with that person, consider what you think and how you feel about that person because you're the one in it and living it. I am still looking for the one at this point in my life. I would say the relationships I've been in personally have been more based on lust, how we felt about one another sexually, from relationships and flings to encounters, but they've never formed into anything because there was no substance besides that. You may be asking me, "Do you believe you will meet your love? Or do you believe you have already met her?" Part of me wants to say I haven't met her, but another believes I have already met her. To all the fellas out there, if you base your relationship on sex, it's almost always a recipe for disaster; it never works out in the long run.

I don't claim to be a perfect person because I am not. We all have inconsistencies, flaws, sin, and things that make us who we are. As I have gone through the years, I have made an effort to lay it all out on the table and be bold and speak the truth, because people will judge you and me anyways. Why not go down to the mirror of reality and speak the truth into your life, rather than keeping it bottled up, waiting on a rainy day?

The story I mentioned above plays into this, as does being in the hospital with blood clots, but when I hit rock bottom and went off the deep end, I had so many things come against me all at once from relationships to family. It was like a sea of fire heading in my direction, and when it got to this point, I had never felt so alone in my life. I was contemplating ending my life. I knew a spot where I would drive my truck off because I knew I wasn't coming back; I would be better off dead. At that time, I remember my grandpa Frank in heaven speaking to me and reminding me of all those weekends we spent together, talking about the love of Jesus. If I hadn't had him and Jesus in my life from day one, I'm not sure if I would have made it because there were so many dark days when the pain overtook my life. I wished for it to be over.

It's not like I've ever been that bad of a son. I've never been in trouble with the law, never smoked drugs, never stuck needles in my arm, and never tried stuff most children try out. I have smoked the odd cigarette, ripped the cigars, drank tequila and whiskey from time to time, and done some dumb things with weight-loss drugs. Over time though, I have learned to forgive people who hurt me because it has helped me move forward. I can't remain in that space where the pain takes over. It never did me any good, nor would it allow me to heal. I have decided to accept people for how they are; I have prayed that someday they will come around, but at the same time, I'm not going to waste any more time trying to fix it. They have to want to do it for themselves. The man I strive to be like is my grandpa Frank Enright; he was one of the kindest people you would ever meet but he also stood up for what he believed in. What made him so special was that he knew God, and he knew that any problem could be solved with the proper steps if both individuals were willing to work it out. He also knew some completely unacceptable things, and he knew when to move on. I don't buy that old story someone may be telling you, "Oh, I can't change." I'm like, "That's the biggest bunch of bullshit I've ever heard." If people want to change, they will find a way to make a change, but they have to do it for themselves, not anyone else.

So, what led up to all these negative thoughts? I believe that these negative thoughts were a result of all the verbal abuse I encountered over the years from various people. The thing about verbal abuse is that it stays with you because words are power. This will happen if someone tells you over the years that "You will never amount to anything. You're not as articulate as other people. How dare you try to do something like that? If it doesn't work out, you know you will have to do something else." It's like, "No, go piss off and fly a kite."

I'm going to get done what God has planned for my life. People will come out of the woodwork when you have a dream or walk into the unknown. I have had many people shit on me over the years, and the sad reality is it's usually not even strangers; it's the people who are the closest to me. Do something great and see who claps for you; you will have your answer after that.

I had blood clots in the same leg on previous occasions; this big one wasn't coincidental. I was visiting my blood doctor at a university-run hospital. I showed up and met with her, and she decided she wanted to take me off the blood thinners. I said, "Fantastic," because the blood thinner I was taking was warfarin, and the side effects were wild. I was lost on cloud nine most days. But after six months off the blood thinners, I ended up in the hospital fighting for my life in the ICU for close to a month. When I left the hospital, I remember the next four months were a nightmare. Everything I did was like running a marathon. I was slurring my words heavily from having the stroke. It took about a year to feel somewhat normal again, and when I returned to the hospital to visit my blood doctor after this unfolded, the first thing she said to me was, "What happened?" I was like, "What do you mean what happened? You took me off the blood thinners, and this happened." I had never seen such fear on someone's face drop in the matter of a second. I was like, "Don't worry; I forgive you as Jesus has forgiven me." After that, it was almost like she was gasping for air. A sigh of relief rushed into her heart. Guess what, she is way more educated than me, but this time she knew she had made a mistake. But I forgave her so I could move on with my life. We can break the chains of bitterness, hate, and resentment when we forgive.

To this day, what makes me happy is personal development, knowing Jesus, helping people, being a significant person, going fast like Ricky Bobby, and various physical activities. I've taken courses, read books, and studied this stuff for a very long time now. From motivational, spiritual, to religious, and from TV, movies, music videos, to commercials, I've been like a sponge in how the human mind works and in knowing if someone is in character or is breaking character and is full of crap. I am the type of person who will go out of their way for someone. I am a very passionate person. I am well aware of everything around me. I have seen people do one dumb thing after another, but it gets to the point where they have to start helping themselves, not you always being there for them. There is usually meaning and purpose behind everything I do, but when we can positively touch someone's life, that's where it hits home for me. It brings me a great sense of joy when something I was able to do could give another person some hope and joy in their own life. But like anything in life, life is hard. It will be an up-and-down roller coaster. I wish I could tell you if you read this book, you will have this everlasting fire in you. Life isn't constantly a thrill; it will require daily action and work on yourself to get to where you want to go in anything you're doing. But with that said, have a positive attitude throughout the process and love people unconditionally when they do something to hurt you. Understanding what they're doing and not taking it personally will separate you from the "kind of" attitude to the "I must do this no matter what" attitude. I pity people still going on about things that happened ten years ago; why do that to yourself? Why relive that pain for yourself? At the end of the day, it's only hurting you, not them. And you may be saying, "How do I get the ball rolling?" Ask yourself this first: "How is my prayer life?" Prayer plays a significant role in people's self-reflection and in knowing how to fix the problem and move forward. When you can pray, I guarantee you that it will plant a seed inside of you to go out and live an unstoppable life rather than worrying about what could happen. Being told the word "No" really helped me realize this at a young age. You will get knocked down a lot through life.

When I was twelve years old, I started acting in TV, commercials, movies, and music video's I did it until I was twenty-five years old, going to audition after audition and failing time after time. The first commercial I ever landed was a football commercial. The premise was that I was in a school spelling bee and had to spell the word "facsimile." Then, after I spelled it correctly, a famous football quarterback at the time ran and dumped a cooler of water meant to look like an energy drink over my head. This was one of the most incredible experiences of my life. I met him and his family and got an autographed jersey at the end of the day. He was a great and super-friendly guy. I remember I was also doing a photoshoot for a magazine that day, and it wasn't going that great. The football player came in and yelled, "Smile, Man," and immediately after that, everything in that photoshoot started going according to plan.

As the years went by, I did many things from TV, movies, commercials, to music, etc. I never landed any significant role. As I kept going through the process, the weirder it got, and I started to realize how many messed up things were being shown to me through various situations and people; it got to the point where I was getting sick and tired of all the fake things I saw going on, and it made me realize it's not the way I want to live.

Hey, it might not happen for everyone, but it's what I experienced. What I enjoyed about acting, though, was the creativity, taking a character and making it believable for the audience, and also the level of memory I developed by reading scripts and having to memorize so many lines and situations throughout the scenes. I also learned how to be comfortable speaking in front of a lot of people, and I learned how to spot someone's bullshit from a mile away. You may be wondering why I stopped. I guess you could say I was burned out playing different roles and playing different characters. That old saying about the definition of insanity is doing the same thing and expecting a different result. Well, I was sick and tired of being sick and tired. I was sick and tired of people looking from the outside in, saying, "Oh, the acting must be lucrative." Yah, when you're getting parts, but when you're not, it's an uphill battle.

I have had many experiences that made me happy and unhappy, but I have never experienced any greater thing in my life than coming to God. His love for us and joy will create a seed of happiness in every area of our lives. He will help us understand how to look at life from a different perspective. It's a love that's hard to describe to someone else, because it is so personal. When we realize that God loves us unconditionally through all our mistakes, flaws, and inconsistencies, being able to live the life that he intended for us will hit close to home. This will happen when we can finally find that thing we were created to do. When you are really into something, ask yourself how much you know about that topic. I am probably willing to bet that you are like a book of knowledge about that subject, but let me ask you this: Why haven't you been pursuing it? Why haven't you taken that leap of faith and decided to believe that you always had the right stuff and that nothing is impossible with God on your side? Everything is there for you to discover. What would it mean if you could live your best life right now? What would it mean if you could have this unstoppable mindset where anything is possible for your life with the right work ethic and God? How would that make you feel? I would bet, that it would light this fire of greatness you have always wanted to discover. Understand this about the devil, because the devil lies in the details: For most people, the devil lies at your doorstep. He will show up in your thoughts and on your way to work. He will show up in your home. Every negative thing has been a reflection of the devil trying to keep us contained so we cannot move forward. If he can do that, he will have anyone's life right where he wants it. Also, when we look at society, it's not cool to be positive. How often have you watched the news and felt like you were ready to go out and tackle the world after? Does it rarely happen? Life is like a garden: it will let you reap what you sow. It's like going out tomorrow and saying, "Well, it's going to be a shit day. It's cold out." Fuck this kind of attitude. How well do you think your day will go after all that negative talk? Whether we plant a seed of positivity or a source of negativity, we will get back whatever we plant. You might have planted a seed of something negative, then the more you talk about it, the bigger it becomes; this little mulberry bush might be a full-blown redwood tree now in your mind by the thoughts and things you have been telling yourself about this particular subject or person. The devil loves to keep us all like that. Smack him back and say, "Not today or any day."

But also surround yourself with positive, happy, kind, funny people. I don't have any time to hang out with negative, toxic people. It wastes my time and energy and limits me from moving forward on the things God has planned for my life. Love conquers all; what we choose to focus on will tell us a lot about ourselves and allow us to manifest into our minds by what we choose to focus on. There is no perfect person in this world. We are all flawed; that's why the negative usually outweighs the positive in most cases. The thing I look at is this: How do I react to it? Am I going to let everything go wrong with the world right now affect me? Or am I going to stand and fight no matter what? Understand that this will require daily work and action on yourself if you want to get to that place of positivity in your life. There is a level of importance in significant living and being that once-in-a-lifetime person for other people. Success is great, and you can do many things with it, but it won't help you be fulfilled because success is all about us. However, being a significant person is about other people. When I got my new car, I went and did the deal by myself and took the keys by myself. It was great for a short period. Sure, I was excited at the moment, but eventually, all that thrill that I initially felt when I first got it wore off. The moral of the story is that if you are searching for happiness through material things, though I hate to break it to you, it will be a never-ending cycle. About a year later, a new model will come out that shows more prestige than your car, so then subconsciously you think, "Mine doesn't carry as much value as this new model." What we have to understand when it comes to material things, things that society claims will make us a better person, is that it's all ego driven. You will say, "Oh, if I do this, then what will this person think of me? If I get this big house, what will I look like as a status symbol to other people?" Others will be looking from the outside, going "Oh, wow! Their life must be remarkable by what they have been able to attain in a material aspect." And suppose you hang out with certain people. Others may think, "If this person hangs out with them, they must be important. If this person does this, they must be highly valued, or their significant other is physically attractive. Their life must be all figured out in the sex department." For me, in regard to a romantic relationship, I look at a person's depth. I like to peel back all the layers of someone who wants to get to know themselves deeply. I like going to the hard conversations so we can get to know each other at the core. I am a very passionate person, and many people would call me aggressive, and some frown on that. I'm here once, one time only, so why not make an effort to get to the core root of things and get to the truth at the end of the day? Why fear? It's like seeing someone get mad at someone for something they did that doesn't involve them, but quickly judging them because of disagreeing with what was done or said. Understand that if you judge, you shall be considered for judgment. Before you think about why someone did what they did, ask yourself: "I wonder what this meant for this person, what this meant for themselves, and why they did that?" Because at the end of the day, we don't know what's going on in someone's life unless they decide to open up to us about what's happening.

I'm a very blunt person. I tell it like it is because I understand that as long as I keep doing this, the more I will keep growing as a person and discovering stuff about myself. But there is also a way of saying it so that you don't come off like a jerk; it's not what you say but how you say it. We live in a texting world where most people would rather text someone to try to find a solution. Meanwhile, that never works at the end of the day. The only thing that will do justice is if you have a good old-fashioned conversation with that person, because nothing beats seeing someone in person rather than through a phone or a video call per say. You can express your affection, especially when it comes to love in general and in any relationship, but there is nothing like saying it and showing it in person. People will feel your energy at the end of the day and see that you genuinely care. You can be that once-in-a-lifetime person for someone else. When I wake up every day, I choose to be a significant person. How can I impact someone in a positive way to help them get past barriers and beliefs they might have for themselves? To me, there is no more incredible feeling than doing something for someone else and giving them a sense of happiness in their own life. You will know that you brought some joy to their life; you gave some hope and some peace. They just needed the right person to come along to remind them of how special a person they are rather than feeling down and out about themselves. Strive to be a once-in-a-lifetime person, and you are one of one. When people look at you, one in a million is great, but being able to be that one person who can genuinely help someone with what they are going through like no one else can, at the end of the day, is going to be a pretty special feeling. Know that what you do can impact someone in such an everlasting, unstoppable way. Others can get to the place of happiness within themselves by something that you were able to touch them with along the way.

Understand that through your walk, people need to see that you care. Over time, people will start to look at how you have invested in the relationship, and how committed you are to show up when the time comes, because in today's society, we need more people to care and have a loving personality where you can express your love through different situations. This can be any relationship. Let that person know that you care, you want to help, you want to grow, and you want to have the same love being shown in your life just as much as you show love for them. Love will conquer everything at the end of the day. For every negative thing you come up against, there will always be some form of love waiting to take over for the current pain. You are amazing. Like God always says, "I will always give you somebody." Understand that there is no love like God's love. The amount of love he gives us even when we do wrong, even when we don't understand, is an unconditional love that surpasses any love we will experience here on Earth. We all have flaws, we all have sinned, we aren't perfect. Just when we think something is going all smooth, there will be something right there to get us frustrated and upset. We need to realize how we react to these situations so that they don't consume us and take over our life. Ask yourself how many thoughts come into your mind every single day. I guarantee you that the negative thoughts will try to take over your mind if you let them. What if you could wake up every day and live in a positive state of mind where the happiness keeps pouring into your heart so that the love in your life can take over for good? How would that make you feel at the end of the day? Understand that these exposures will get into our thoughts. What are you allowing to come into this great mind of yours every day? Ask yourself: "Are these things I'm allowing into my mind going to benefit my life in any way, shape, or form?" What if you could wake up and listen, read, or watch something positive when you first rise? What do you think it would do for your health and development over time if you could program your brain when you first wake up to let all these positive thoughts flow abundantly into your life? How do you think, over time, this would affect your life? I guarantee it would plant a seed of positivity in your life, but the choice is yours. Is this something for you? The moral of the story is to do what makes you happy with your life. Nothing will compare when you genuinely start expressing that gift you were given at birth from God. Expressing your gift is crucial to begin living your true self and discovering who you are.

I know people who have the most random job you could think of, and they are successful because they love what they do. They are connected to what they do, and they usually reap the rewards that come with being successful. When you love something, you are willing to go above and beyond what's necessary. You have a fire to push the limits, and it almost becomes game overtime or a chess match, you could say, to make strategic moves and get to the next level. I laugh when people get jealous of other people for being good at something. Maybe this person has recognized their gift. Maybe they are living in their talent. If you are worried about what someone else is doing, you're going to waste a lot of time pondering and questioning what you are great at. We all have something we were born to do, whether someone tells us or not. The mission is too critical to not start expressing what you are genuinely great at, because what you are genuinely great at can help someone for the greater good and touch them in a positive way. You have to be willing to take a jump. I'm not telling you to run out and quit your job tomorrow. What I am telling you, though, is to start doing what you love part-time until it becomes a full-time thing. Even if you don't receive a short-term reward, long-term wins are always worth it in the big picture. Nothing worth having comes easily. Like the old saying, easy come, easy go, but you need to be able to discover that thing that is running deep down in your bones, that thing you are obsessed about at the end of the day. When you talk about it, you get fired up about it in a positive way. We need more people living in their gift and being happy. Progressing a little bit each day will ultimately lead to happiness. For example, think about what you truly love. What is the emotion you feel when you think about this particular thing? How much energy do you have after the fact compared to when you started? When we love doing something, it will give us power and ultimately feed a desire to keep going.

Be passionate. Be committed, stick with the process, and understand there will be ups and downs no matter what. Never give up on your dream at any point. Don't think about how crazy it sounds to other people, because when we look for approval, we look to God. After all, there will be nothing that can compare when you seek support from God and allow him to show up in your life.

For more information, and for speaking services, visit my website: www.awakenthephoenix.global. We strive to help people get past anything they are going through in their life to get to their definition of happiness. Check out my Instagram page, awakenthephoenix_global, for videos and writeups that can be valuable tools for your life to help you become that significant person in someone else's life and the universe. Also, be a once-in-a-lifetime person for others. When others see the clouds in their life, be that person to show them the sunlight. Let them know that you love them simply for who they are. My message to you is to go out there and be a significant, unstoppable, everlasting, gifted, faithful, forgiving, kind, relentless, bold, and truth-seeking believer, evolver, and striver. Be a hungry, one-of-one loving person so that we can not only see the gift that you can share with us but also how many lives you will be able to touch along the way. This is Brett Andrew Miller. Have a great day.

CPSIA information can be obtained
at www.ICGtesting.com
Printed in the USA
LVHW020037121122
732945LV00003B/72

9 780228 881421

HowExpert Presents

Mini Horror Fiction Writing Guide

7 Steps To Writing Horror Fiction For Fun

HowExpert with Randal Schaffer

For more tips related to this topic, visit HowExpert.com/horrorfiction.

Recommended Resources

- HowExpert.com – Quick 'How To' Guides on All Topics from A to Z by Everyday Experts.
- HowExpert.com/free – Free HowExpert Email Newsletter.
- HowExpert.com/books – HowExpert Books
- HowExpert.com/courses – HowExpert Courses
- HowExpert.com/membership – HowExpert Membership Site
- HowExpert.com/writers – Write About Your #1 Passion/Knowledge/Expertise & Become a HowExpert Author.
- HowExpert.com/resources – Additional HowExpert Recommended Resources
- YouTube.com/HowExpert – Subscribe to HowExpert YouTube.
- Instagram.com/HowExpert – Follow HowExpert on Instagram.
- Facebook.com/HowExpert – Follow HowExpert on Facebook.

Table of Contents

INTRODUCTION

Thank you for downloading this instructure on writing effective horror fiction.

Many people who love and write horror stories dream of gaining the wealth and fame of Stephen King, Dean Koontz, or Clive Barker. I am not going to promise that you will, for several reasons. First off, each of these people are unique talents, just as you are. Second, they each have their own vision and point of view, just like you do. Third, writing with the objective of being a best-selling author is a fool's errand. Any story that you write should be written for one reason only – because you love the genre, the story, and the characters. In this day and age, when literally anyone can write a story and publish it on Amazon, there's a lot of competition for the reader's eye and dollar. This increase in competition makes it increasingly difficult to be a million-seller.

What this book will do is teach you, using examples from literature, cinema and TV, how to write a horror story that people will want to read. It will teach you how to write a compelling story by helping you create a world that your readers will want to inhabit by drawing believable, sympathetic characters, making an environment that the reader will be comfortable in for the length of your story, and creating a series of events that will keep your readers' eyes glued to the screen until you're done with them. If you've done it right, they'll be glad that they're out at the end. It will not teach you the basics of story craft and construction: if you have the eye of a professional writer, you've already mastered these anyway.

The three most important tips, however, are read, read, and finally, READ. Don't limit yourself to the "best-sellers". In his excellent book *On Writing: A Memoir of the Craft*, Stephen King says, "If you don't have the time to read, then you don't have the time (or tools) to write." I have this phrase as a computer desktop wallpaper just to remind myself, although I am a voracious reader. Read the good, read the bad, and read the ugly. Read horror and other genres alike. Not only will this teach you how to write engrossing horror, it will also teach you some pitfalls to avoid which will prevent people from wanting to read your material in the future.

So if you're ready, follow me as I lead you down the dark and twisting path of good horror fiction, and, hopefully, come out the other side a better story teller.

Randal Schaffer (contributing author for HowExpert.com)

STEP 1: CHOOSING A TOPIC

When it comes to writing fiction, especially genre fiction like horror, you need to decide what your topic will be. This is a step that too many writers don't take at the very beginning of their work, leading to stories that meander from lane to lane like a blind drunk on a freeway. Even if your story contains several sub-topics, there should be one overarching storyline that ties them all together. An excellent example of this is the book *Boy's Life* by Robert R. McCammon. The book contains a ghost, a ghost dog, a dinosaur, the death of a bicycle, but always comes back to the central story of a murder mystery.

Pick a Monster, Any Monster

In horror fiction, your monster (even if that monster is human) will be at the center of the story, perhaps even more important than your protagonist.

There are certain monster archetypes that we see again and again in horror fiction, used to one degree of success or another. There's the vampire (*Dracula*, *'Salem's Lot*, and Brian Lumley's *Necroscope* series among others), the werecreature (*Silver Bullet* and any number of "wolfman" films) and the formless "thing" (*Frankenstein*, *The Thing*, and any of Lovecraft's terrors from beyond space). To a lesser degree there are also mummies, witches, and a favorite of the 80's: the evil child. In addition, then there's the ever-popular human monster, seen as

Norman Bates in *Psycho* or any number of slasher movies that followed it.

Remember that your monster doesn't have to fit into any of these archetypes. The *Silent Hill* series of video games and movies featured creatures that aren't recognizable as anything, and yet still manage to be threatening and scary.

The important thing to remember about your monster is that it should neither be too easy to dispose of, nor so overwhelmingly powerful that no human force can overcome it. The werecreature, for instance, is done away with by a shot from a silver or holy bullet. Stephen King showed the difficulties of making an effective silver bullet in his novella *Cycle of the Werewolf*, which became the movie *Silver Bullet*. At the other end of the spectrum, you have the angel from Clive Barker's *Weaveworld* and anything by H. P. Lovecraft.

Regarding Lovecraft, as much as you may enjoy his fiction, this type of story struggles for believability today. As "Cthulu", "Hastur", and "the Old Ones" have become a part of our common horror language, it should be noted that they are essentially unbeatable, and Lovecraft also took shortcuts on describing the monsters. No reader today would allow you to get away with a monster that simply drives the protagonist mad with a glimpse. Instead, you want to create a monster that the reader can envision, even if the description borders on vague and thus allows the reader to draw their own conclusions as to what it looks like. Barker's angel in *Weaveworld*, for example, is described as being "all geometry". Above all, your monster should be frightening, even if it's just the photo department guy at your local store (*One Hour Photo*), the hotel clerk (*Psycho*), or the grandparents (*The Visit*). As a matter of fact, if you're going to have a human monster, the blander they start out, the better. Looking at all three aforementioned examples, the human monsters start the story or film seeming so benign that you could never imagine them being a threat. When we meet Norman Bates at the beginning of *Psycho*, he just seems like kind of the nerdy, bumbling boy next door. This differs from, say, Ed Gein, about whom many films have been made, including *The Texas Chainsaw Massacre*. When you meet a guy wearing a human skin mask and sitting in a chair made out of human bones, you know that you're courting trouble by hanging out with him.

Making What's Old New Again

One of the biggest problems with genre fiction in general, as well as horror fiction in specific, is that it sometimes seems that everything's been done. Universal's "Famous Monsters" had so many movies made about them from the thirties to the fifties that they ultimately wound up being self-parodies, and only living on as *Abbot and Costello Meet the Monsters*.

The best way to succeed here is to reinvent the genre. John Carpenter is credited with creating the slasher genre, for instance, with his 1978 film *Halloween*. But if you look back in cinema history, you see the human monster going back in film as far as 1931 with Fritz Lang's M. When Stephen King decided to reignite the vampire genre with *'Salem's Lot*, he approached it from the perspective of placing the monsters in the modern era where you could just use the phone to call for help or drive away in your car. Probably the most recent archetype is the zombie, credited to George Romero's *Night of the Living Dead* in 1968. Romero, however, never used the term "zombie" or thought of his creatures as such. He simply referred to them as "ghouls".

Another way to breathe life into an old story is to take the story in a new direction or from a new perspective. Tell the story, for instance, from the monster's point of view, for example. This only really works, however, if your monster is in some way sympathetic. Telling a story from the point of view of *The Blob*, for instance, may be an insurmountable chore, since it's basically just a big eating machine. You can also tell the story from the point of view of one of the subsidiary characters. Personally, I'd love the see the *Dracula* story told from the point of view of his human servant Renfield. Or you can take the established story and characters and do something totally new with them, as I've done in my novella *Lady Frankenstein's Lover*. The caution here is that you want the established characters to remain true to how they were in the original book. In genre fiction, this is referred to as "canon". For instance, you don't necessarily want to see Victor Frankenstein helping little old ladies across the street or helping out at a soup kitchen. An excellent example of this, although done strictly for laughs, was Mel Brooks' *Young Frankenstein*.

Starting Your Journey

Lao Tzu said, "The journey of a thousand miles starts with a single step." Similarly, your journey through darkness has to begin with an opening word, sentence, paragraph, or chapter. I will personally give a book one chapter to capture my attention. The sooner that you have the reader hooked, the happier they will be to let you lead them on your path of terror. If they have to slog through three chapters of hearing about how the antagonist's grandmother loved to do needlepoint, you'll probably lose them. There is an annual contest called the Bulwer-Lytton Fiction Contest that awards a prize of "a pittance" for the worse opening lines in fiction. The award is named in honor of Edward George Bulwer-Lytton who, in his novel Paul Clifford, created the now-archetypal bad first line of a novel: "It was a dark and stormy night". If you'd like to see some things to avoid, their website, bulwer-lytton.com is a great resource.

By the same token, unless you intend to do a lot of backing and filling, you don't want to immediately drop the reader into the middle of an intense action scene, or start with the death (or impending death) of the protagonist. In the 1950 and 1988 film versions of *D. O. A.*, for example, the protagonist starts the film off poisoned and on death's door, and must review his past to figure out who poisoned him and why. This can be an effective tool, but only if handled well and gently.

STEP 2: SETTING THE SETTING

Once you have the theme of your story firmly in mind, the next thing that you have to decide is where and when to set it. Do you want your protagonist to be isolated or surrounded by others who can help him or her, even if they only serve the purpose of sacrificing themselves so that your protagonist can live to the end. Are they surrounded by people who love and support them, or by mobs of angry villagers that only want their blood? The setting of your story can go a long way to creating the suspense and horror of your story, or, if handled wrong, completely destroy it.

Gothic

The classic gothic horror story is, of course, Bram Stoker's *Dracula*. Old, cob-web filled castles, a boat at high sea with all deckhands found dead, and an isolated country estate. If you look up the definition of gothic in the dictionary, you're likely to find *Dracula*.

The gothic setting is pre-industrial. No phones, no cars, no first responders. It's very easy to create a feeling of dread in a gothic setting due to your protagonist being stuck in a certain situation. The fastest mode of transport that they have is literal horse power, which can be done away with fairly easily. This leaves your protagonist alone, or with just the people around him or her, to face the horror.

The biggest things to be cautious of when using a gothic setting are to make sure that your references are correct for the setting you're using, and to bring some fresh perspective to the setting itself. Although not gothic or horror, the prime example of an anachronism(a chronological inconsistency) can be found in Shakespeare's *Julius Caesar*, where a clock can be heard striking in ancient Rome, hundreds of years before the invention of mechanical clocks.

Modern

As the 21st century progresses, less and less horror fiction is being placed in a gothic or sci-fi setting, and more of it is being set in modern times: in the world that we all know. There is a certain effectiveness given to horror if it could be happening in your neighborhood, on your street, or in your living room, rather than in Dracula's castle or a space station circling a distant sun.

By placing the horror story in a modern setting, you are quite literally placing your reader directly in the middle of it. You are telling them, "This is what's happening right now in the house next door to you".

The modern setting is also useful for presenting challenges both for your characters and for you as a writer. As I stated in the introduction to this section, how can you create peril for your character if they can simply get in a car and drive away? Different authors handle this in a variety of ways. Steve Niles, in his graphic novel *30 Days of Night*, set his story in Point Barrow, Alaska. No roads connect Point Barrow to the rest of the state and (at least in the graphic novel and film) no airplane leaves the airstrip during the titular 30 days of night. In *Cujo*, Stephen King simply broke the car in question. A mother and her child are stuck outside of their mechanic's house in a car that won't start, being menaced by a rabid Saint Bernard. It is always good to challenge yourself as a writer; to play a game of "What if?" with yourself, and creating menace in a modern setting is a terrific way to do that.

Sci-Fi

The sci-fi horror story has been a staple of literature since at least the 19th century, and cinema since at least 1930, when *Frankenstein* was introduced in each form. Although Mary Shelley considered her story a tale of cautionary science and not horror, and Frankenstein's creature is arguably the most sympathetic monster in history, both the book and the film are certainly horrific, even if you simply view it from the perspective of how the monster was treated by society.

In many ways, the sci-fi setting can be viewed as an alternate gothic setting. Aren't the astronauts on the Nostromo in *Alien* every bit as isolated as Jonathan Harker was at Castle Dracula? Communication would take days instead of seconds, and simply leaving the ship would require placing yourself in suspended animation. No easy escape, in other words.

The real advantage to the sci-fi setting is that you're pretty much free to go anywhere you want with the story. For example, in a gothic or modern setting, if you wanted your protagonist to discover a new plant that would help him or her defeat the monster, you'd have a much harder time making it believable than if you could simply place both them and the monster on an alien planet where the needed plant already exists. Nothing is off-limits nor out of bounds in a sci-fi setting, as long as the story follows the logic that you, as the creator, set up for it. For example, if you want to have your protagonist escape from the monster by jumping 20 feet straight up to a ledge, you can do that, as long as you've already established that the planet they're on has a low enough gravity to make it possible. If your planet has "earth-normal" gravity, then that escape isn't possible, and you'd have to come up with some kind of alternate plan. Jet boots, anyone?

STEP 3: MAKING PEOPLE

Writer, meet character. Character, meet writer.

Your characters should be real enough to you to require that kind of introduction. They should live and breathe not just with you, but glued to your side like a bunch of conjoined twins.

The best way to do this is to create an entire back-story for your character, whether it will be used expressly in the story or not. This is where my example of grandma's needlepoint will come in handy. It may not be featured in the story, but you'll know that everything that grandma says or does is something that would be said and done by an old lady who does needlepoint. For instance, when I think of that character, I think of a little old lady who inserts the word "dear" into each sentence somewhere. There are basically three types of characters who will appear in your story: the protagonist, the antagonist, and... everyone else.

The Protagonist

The protagonist is your main character. This is the person that you want everyone to fall in love with so that they will follow the character through the entire story. Robert Bloch pulled perhaps the greatest trick on readers the world over when he had Marion Crane killed less than halfway through the novel *Psycho*. *Psycho* may be viewed as the first novel with no real protagonist, unless you consider Norman Bates the protagonist, and his psyche-dwelling mother the antagonist.

When I have the conversation with other writers, they point out that there are some books and movies with more than one protagonist. Although I can understand that argument, I would argue that there is one that is more important than the others, unless you're telling a massive *Game of Thrones* type story, switching from one POV to another, and giving each approximately the same amount of time. But even there, you could say that the protagonist is the Stark family as a unit. Stephen King's *It* is one of the rare occasions where you have a group of protagonists, all of approximately equal value to the story, with each serving a vital role. But even this is a rather extreme exception to the rule. Yes, *Scooby Doo* has an entire team of protagonists, but aren't they all there ultimately to carry Scooby snacks for the dog?

Also, please don't misconstrue my statement that the protagonist has to be someone that the reader will fall in love with. You can absolutely have a hateful protagonist: Frank Underwood in *House of Cards* or Archie Bunker in *All in the Family*, for instance. They are literally characters that you love to hate. Although you don't love or necessarily even LIKE these characters, you are compelled to continue watching simply to see what kind of mischief they get up to. But this is a more difficult proposition in horror fiction than it is in political drama or comedy. Let's face it, if Frank Underwood were trapped on the Nostromo, we'd pretty much all be rooting for the xenomorph to get him. If things work out badly for the protagonist, you want the reader to be moved to tears of sadness as opposed to whoops of joy.

The Antagonist

In horror fiction, I use the phrase "the monster" to generically mean the antagonist. The antagonist is the motor of your story, the one who creates an interesting story for your protagonist. No one (at least, no one that I know) wants to read a story about a character who sits on his couch watching TV all day for his entire life until he dies peacefully of old age. Give me some conflict! That's why the antagonist exists.

Your antagonist can be just about anyone or anything. In the Clive Barker story *The Body Politic*, the antagonist is the hands of the protagonist, rebelling against the rest of the body. Peter Merideth's short story *The Pen* features an antagonist that is... well... a pen. An ink pen. Yes, really. There is no limit, especially when you utilize a sci-fi setting to what the antagonist can be. But seriously, if you're going to follow the examples of Barker or Meredith and make your antagonist something bizarre like that, you had better have a damned compelling story to tell in order for the reader to take the antagonist seriously. Because, unless you're writing a comedy like *Despicable Me*, you want your reader to do so.

The biggest decision that you need to make on your antagonist is how much you want your reader to feel for them. Do you want mindless killing machines that require no sympathy like Pyramid Head in the *Silent Hill* franchise, or do you want pathetic, misunderstood monsters as seen in *Frankenstein* or *The Phantom of the Opera*? This will help you decide how complex you want your story to be. If your antagonist is a dude in a hockey mask with an axe, your story is simple: protagonist running from antagonist. If your antagonist is a lonely, mentally ill young man who was abused and possibly molested by his mother before he ultimately killed her, than you have a much more detailed story to tell. This is why books and films like *Frankenstein* and *Psycho* have had such long and prosperous lives: they are not simple stories.

Of course, you also have to decide if you want your antagonist to win. It is possible to drag a protagonist through hell, only to have them die or worse at the end. Sam Raimi's film *Drag Me to Hell* is a great example of this. Think of the books that you've read or the movies that you've seen where the bad guys defeat the good guys at the end. People sometimes forget that this was the ending of the original *Nightmare on Elm Street* before it became a huge hit and New Line decided that it should be a franchise.

Cannon Fodder/Nameless Rabble/Angry Villagers

Now, you have the nameless ranks of people who will flesh out the story. The parents, children, needlepointing grandmas, shopkeepers, grumpy neighbors and refrigerator repairmen. The people who surround the protagonist. Some can be supportive, such as the girlfriend and best friend of the protagonist in Barry Lyga's *I Hunt Killers* trilogy, or some can just be cannon fodder, there to feed the monster, like almost any of the campers in any of the Friday the 13th movies.

The primary job of your secondary characters is to fill space in one way or another, or to move the story along. For example, without the detective Arbogast or Marion's sister Lila in *Psycho,* the story would have come to a screeching halt after Marion's death. Norman would have rolled her car into the swamp, everyone back home would have assumed that she simply took the money and ran, and that would have been it.

But this doesn't mean that you can skimp on these characters, either. Although you don't need to develop the kind of full backstory for them that you do for the protagonist, they have to be more than scenery. You do have to develop them fully, for whatever their function is. Take the campers in Friday the 13th as an example of what NOT to do in fiction. Slasher films are also called "body factory films" because all they do is introduce a character to be killed later. After Kevin Bacon got his show business start being paddled in the John Landis comedy *Animal House*, he decided that a good career move would be to appear as the cannon fodder character "Jack" in Friday the 13th. Jack has more character development than most of the other campers and counselors in the film: he's in a wheelchair. But that's it. They all talk the same, do the same things, have the same motivation, and die at the hands of Jason or Mrs. Voorhees, depending on the film. That's simply not good enough. Let's say that you have a grandmother in your book who will ultimately die defending the protagonist. Her part is small. So do we need to know that she scrubbed potatoes for a penny in the depression, or helped to build fighter planes in world war two? No. But she DOES have to be an accessible, complete character to the reader, so simply knowing that she does needlepoint, bakes cookies every other day, and includes the word "dear" somewhere in each sentence is plenty.

STEP 4: BUILDING SUSPENSE

A horror story without suspense is completely useless. Suspense is what keeps your readers biting their nails and sitting on the edge of their seat as they turn page after page, unable to put the book down until they find out what happens next. The best way to learn about writing suspense is to watch any Alfred Hitchcock film or interview with the man.

Protagonist in Peril

Of course, the best way to create suspense is to put your protagonist in some sort of peril pretty much constantly throughout the story. Once Michael Myers dispatches the handful of cannon fodder characters in Halloween, what we're left with is Laurie finding herself in one perilous situation after another at Michael's hands until the film is resolved - more or less.

One thing that you want to be careful of, however, if you're writing a series, is to put your protagonist in mortal peril at the end of one story, creating a cliffhanger for the next story. Once you have done this often enough, the reader will no longer believe in the peril, hence the suspense is effectively killed. Series television has done this to death. *Smallville* was a perfect example of all the main characters, including Clark Kent, being put in some sort of mortal peril in the season finale, to be resolved within the first fifteen minutes of the next season's premiere. This can be turned on its head, however. *The Walking Dead* has a great habit of killing its main characters off - although the protagonist, Rick Grimes, plugs right along. *Game of Thrones* had perhaps the greatest reversal of this in its first season when it killed off the person who appeared to be the protagonist of the series, Ned Stark, during the first season finale.

You also need to be careful to resolve the peril in a believable way, or you will lose another type of suspense: the temporary suspension of disbelief that you want your readers to maintain to keep turning those pages. If your character has never used a gun, and you write them finding, loading, and ultimately shooting the monster from fifty feet away - killing it with a single shot, no less - then that will probably be the last of your stories that your readers ever read.

Agreeable Antagonist

We talked a little about the sympathetic antagonist in the chapter about character, but it is possible to create suspense by making your antagonist downright likeable. In Barry Lyga's *I Hunt Killers* trilogy, the antagonist, Billy Dent, is the father of the protagonist, Jasper (Jazz) Dent. And by golly, you LIKE Billy through most of the trilogy. Like most sociopaths, he's a very pleasant guy on the outside. Think of Dexter from Jeff Lindsay's book series or the Showtime TV series of the same name, or any time you see a story about a busted serial killer on the news. Everyone that they interview says the same thing: "He was just the nicest guy..." Think of suspense and true crime writer Ann Rule, who worked for years at a crisis hotline for a guy that she described as "sensitive", who turned out to be serial killer Ted Bundy.

Yes, it's entirely possible to make a likeable monster. As a matter of fact, the more likeable that you make your monster, the more suspense that you're going to create around it and the longer of a "shelf-life" that it has. We are still telling stories about Dracula, Frankenstein and the Phantom of the Opera, whereas most of the monsters from the "faceless killer" era, like Jason Voorhees and Michael Myers may have a string of films pumped out about them in a fairly short period of time, but after that, no one cares anymore. With Michael Myers, director Rob Zombie was able to drum up enough interest in the character to reboot *Halloween* and make one sequel, but interest simply died. There was a reboot of *Friday the 13th*, produced by Michael Bay, but it fared poorly at the box office. Another reboot was planned in 2016, but then was scrapped because of lack of interest. Even Freddy Krueger, one of the most likeable antagonists in film history suffered an ill-fated reboot.

Showing the Bomb

"There is a distinct difference between "suspense" and "surprise," and yet manypictures continually confuse the two. I'll explain what I mean.

We are now having a very innocent little chat. Let's suppose that there is a bomb underneath this table between us. Nothing happens, and then all of a sudden, "Boom!" There is an explosion. The public is surprised, but prior to this surprise, it has seen an absolutely ordinary scene, of no special consequence. Now, let us take a suspense situation. The bomb is underneath the table and the public knows it, probably because they have seen the anarchist place it there. The public is aware the bomb is going to explode at one o'clock and there is a clock in the decor. The public can see that it is a quarter to one. In these conditions, the same innocuous conversation becomes fascinating because the public is participating in the scene. The audience is longing to warn the characters on the screen: "You shouldn't be talking about such trivial matters. There is a bomb beneath you and it is about to explode!""

This quote is from Alfred Hitchcock, the absolute master of suspense. Some would argue that Hitchcock's films aren't horror films, but I would disagree. *Psycho* and *Frenzy* are both classic "slasher" films, and *The Birds* is simply horrifying. What Hitchcock talks about here also differentiates good horror from mediocre, forgettable horror. If you replace the term 'surprise' with 'jump scare', then you have the difference between *Friday the 13th* and *Psycho*. *Friday the 13th* is jump scare after jump scare, with really no suspense being created between the attacks. In *Psycho*, by the time Arbogast and Lila show up, we KNOW that Norman is the killer, and we have the same reaction that he mentions here... we want to yell at them to GET THE HELL AWAY FROM THAT HOUSE!

STEP 5: GRAPHIC GORE OR GORE NO MORE?

The use of gore in horror movies has been under debate since the seventies, with the birth of the slasher film. But the question remains: "Is it good or bad?" And more importantly to you, as a writer, should you use it or not? And if you do, how much is too much? Personally, I think that gore, like sex, or just about anything else, should be used to an amount that serves the story and no more, or else it becomes distracting from the story that you're trying to tell.

Gentle Horror

There are plenty of good horror stories and movies out there that use little or no gore. Think of Shyamalan's *Sixth Sense*: this is a film which creates a pervasive sense of creepiness, as well as a nice twist ending almost entirely without the use of gore. When gore is used, like the little ghost boy who killed himself with his dad's gun, it is entirely in the service of the story.

Psycho is another effective, creepy horror story that employs a very restrained use of gore. You see some blood swirling down the drain when Marion is killed, and a slash on Arbogast's face, but aside from that (and Mother's desiccated corpse), nothing.

The challenge that many authors face is telling an effective horror story without any gore. Yes, it is more difficult. Imagine trying to describe the attack on Marion Crane from *Psycho* without describing the knife penetrating flesh. It is almost a dance to draw a suspenseful, exciting story without wading through blood. But it can be done.

Take the time to note everything else going on in the scene, just from what we see in the movie: you have so much there to draw on. The water washing her body clean with each stroke. The torn shower curtain. The empty look in her eyes after the murder is completed.

Stephen King is an author who can either take gore and use it very effectively (such as his description of the Captain Trips ravaged bodies in *The Stand*) or leave it (*Cujo*). In the latter tale, almost the entire book is a mother and her young son trapped in a disabled car while a rabid Saint Bernard attacks the car, keeping them trapped, on an extremely hot day. Another book where King used gore very sparingly but to great effect was *Misery*. Think of the shock that you felt when Annie Wilkes cut off Paul Sheldon's foot to keep him from running away, or his attack on her at the end of the book. Because these graphic tactics had not been used to that point in the book, they draw extra attention to themselves without being too much.

Body Horror

The nineties saw the birth of a mutated type of horror story: body horror. Movies like *Saw* or *Hostel* told stories that elicited their horror almost entirely from pain inflicted on, or mutilation of, the human body. An argument made in the media at the time was that these types of movies are simply "torture porn", and it's certainly a worthwhile argument. If you think of porn as being singularly fixed on sexual acts; these are certainly movies that are singularly fixed on torture. And, although I am not personally a fan of them, I will say that they do create a certain unease in the conscientious viewer. Stephen King, in his essay on the horror genre, Danse Macabre described this feeling as "terror" rather than "horror", with terror being, as the introduction to the first *Silent Hill* video game puts it, a fear for the flesh.

The main storytelling problem that I see with these types of stories is that, if overused, they're kind of lazy. It's a shortcut. Yes, if you describe in loving detail every cut that your monster inflicts on his victim, then you're certainly going to create that "fear for the flesh" in your readers. Frankly, you can also burn up a lot of words doing it, if you just need to pad your novel. It's certainly easier to create this type of terror than it is to create suspense. And I don't think that the two are mutually exclusive. Body horror can be used effectively along with good suspense to create a tight, compelling story. Lyga's *I Hunt Killers* trilogy is a perfect example of this. He uses a textual trick to help him create suspense; he will end a paragraph with an unresolved scene, and then jump to another character's POV so that we have to wait paragraphs or even chapters to discover the resolution. He is outstanding at "showing the bomb".

Another problem is that most of the characters in these films are cannon fodder, even in regarding the protagonists. If you've seen any of these films, try to think back on the characters. Can you remember any of them? I mean beyond vague information that, for instance, Cary Elwes' character was a doctor? Can you remember their names? Now think of *Alien* or *Psycho* or even *Halloween*. I know that I can bring up several characters from these films and describe at least a good chunk of their backstory in detail.

Bathing in Blood

Countess Elizabeth Bathory is probably not the monster that we all know her as. The reason for this is because actual, verifiable details of her life are few and far between and typically only found in scholarly texts. The LEGENDS about her, however, that she was a vampire who bathed in the blood of virgins in order to keep her young, are constantly circling. These legends even gave us the phrase 'bathed in blood', which I paraphrased for the title of this section.

Although the real furor over gore in films really started in the seventies and became a major issue in the eighties, the use, or perhaps overuse of gore had been around for at least fifteen years prior to then.

There was a genre of horror film that started cropping up in the mid-sixties, usually cheaply-made and heavily dependent on sex, nudity, the gross-out and body horror. Masters of this craft included Herschel Gordon Lewis, Lucio Fulci and Mario Bava. Many of these directors, including the aforementioned, made their films in Europe in order to escape the strict hold that studios had over Hollywood. The most commonly-used name for this subgenre is the "Grindhouse Flick". Robert Rodriguez and Quentin Tarantino made their own mark on this cinematic style with their double-feature movie *Grindhouse*, all the way down to making trailers for other almost-nonexistent grindhouse movies, such as *Werewolf Women of the SS and Machete* (which actually DID become a successful film and even spawned a sequel).

Personally, I have not seen many successful "Grindhouse Novels", but I'm sure that there's a market for them. As a matter of fact, since the entire story would be, like the films, focused on gratuitous sex and violence, there are probably independent writers writing them and self-publishing on Amazon today.

STEP 6: MAKING THE STORY WORK

Okay, so you've got your topic, your setting and your characters in place, and you have a good idea of how to create suspense in your story and what is just the right amount of gore for your tale.

Now we're going to get into the real machinery of the story. The real gears of it. We're going to get into the details of how to actually create the tale that you're trying to tell. We'll talk about how to create a believable, grounded story with characters that your readers will care about.

The Rifle in Chapter 1

"Remove everything that has no relevance to the story. If you say in the first chapter that there is a rifle hanging on the wall, in the second or third chapter it absolutely must go off. If it's not going to be fired, it shouldn't be hanging there."

This quote is from Anton Chekhov, playwright and author. He expanded on this in a letter to Aleksandr Semenovich Lazarev by saying, "It's wrong to make promises that you don't keep."

Stephen King once referred to something similar in talking about writing the "Bachman" book *The Running Man*, when he said that he kept everything that was vital to the story, and everything else he merrily chucked overboard.

In other words, keep only what's necessary when you're writing a genre piece. Trim the lace. If it's not vital to the story, shoot it in the head and leave it for dead by the side of the road. Think back to grandma's needlepoint. Mentioning it once to deepen your character is fine. Describing in loving detail every piece that she ever worked on, unless you're writing a literary novel instead of a genre novel, will simply slow your story down, and leave your reader wondering "So what?" It is, simply, filler. And trust me, the discerning reader of horror stories will recognize that pretty quickly.

An example of a movie that pared everything down to story amazingly well was David Fincher's *Fight Club*. If you're a film buff, when you're done watching the film the first time, you'll be overcome with the desire to turn right around and re-watch it, simply to pick up on all the little notes and flavors that you missed before.

The other side of that coin is the film *Death Proof*, which constituted Quentin Tarantino's half of *Grindhouse*. Somewhere in the middle of all the long conversations about stuff that had no real impact on the story is a pretty good horror film about a monster with a car. When I saw this film in the theater, in the middle of the first of too many long conversations, I was considering a trip to the concession stand because I was bored, and a look around the cinema at the number of people who were fidgeting, whispering to each other and glancing at their watches told me that I was not alone.

Unless boredom is the emotion that you're trying to elicit with your story, merrily chuck it overboard if it's not progressing your story.

Reasonable Actions and Reactions

This is a point where I often get stuck in conversations with friends about movies and books - any type of storytelling, really. With my definition of "reasonable" being "it works in the universe that you've set up in the story", all of your actions and reactions need to be reasonable.

The first time that I saw Tim Burton's *Batman*, I loved it so much that I got back in line immediately, bought another ticket and watched it again. On my way out the second time, I overheard someone else leaving the theater talking about the motivation of the Joker being "unclear". I said "This is a story about a guy who dresses up like a bat and beats the crap out of people. What do you need?" Yes, from a strict storytelling standpoint, the motivations of Jack Nicholson's Joker character were muddy and unclear. That also holds true for most of the other characters in the film. But again, given the universe that was established for this story, that's fine.

You simply want what happens in the story to work within the confines of the story, and are not simply there as filler or to make the story work. In 1998, Michael Bay directed a film about a group of people who had to save the earth from being destroyed by a huge asteroid, called *Armageddon*. I won't harp on this film too much except to say that the star, Bruce Willis, couldn't stop talking about how ridiculous the film was in its commentary. But there is a perfect example of this. The craft that this group of (largely) non-astronauts needs to use to stop the asteroid has a machine gun on top. Think about this for a second. A craft designed to fly in space, and there's a machine gun ON TOP. Why? Well, it turns out that Steve Buscemi needs the machine gun later in the film to shoot his way out of a hangar. If you think about this, it has to pose the question "Then did the people who designed the craft take in the possibility that Steve Buscemi would need something to help him get out of a hangar?" If the answer is "No", which it obviously is, then you have to think of another reason to have a machine gun on the top of the craft, and then... thank God it was there when Buscemi needed it.

There's actually a fairly easy trick to fixing this problem. Think back to my example of a protagonist who has never held or fired a gun, and suddenly you need them to be Quick Draw McGraw to dispatch the monster with a dead-eye shot. Easy fix? Simply go back to an earlier chapter (the earlier the better, so that it doesn't feel plugged in at the last moment) and have the protagonist reminisce about how his or her dad would regularly take them out into the back forty for firearm lessons, until they could load, handle, and shoot a gun like a pro.

Caring for Your Characters

Finally, the ultimate part of telling your story: your characters. We spoke earlier about how your characters should be real to you. They should be living, breathing people inhabiting your immediate space. My characters are so real to me that, if I'm stuck in a story, I can simply have a mental conversation with one of them to resolve the stuck spot.

The biggest secret to this is to not skimp on your character's actions in the story, especially the protagonist. I don't mean spend three pages describing the ingrown toenails and bunions on the character's feet and the tiredness of his leg muscles when he takes a step. Doing that is simply filler, or a sign that you're reading the Tolkien novel *The Two Towers*. What I mean is to have your characters go on long, expositional jaunts as they move through your story. A real advantage of writing a story over a screenplay is that if a character simply thinks about something, it can engage a reader but will bore a viewer silly, unless you're going to go the Shakespeare route and include soliloquies, which opens its own bucket of worms.

I'm going to return to Lyga's *I Hunt Killers* trilogy here. The protagonist, Jazz, spends much of the book agonizing, almost on a level with Hamlet. He agonizes over everything that he does, wondering if it's because it's what he really wants to do, or if he's doing it because he's somehow messed up mentally because his dad was a serial killer. He agonizes over the morality of having friends because he never knows when he might start following the same road. He agonizes over the fact that his girlfriend is African American, unsure if he loves her for her, or just considers her "safe" since his dad never murdered an African American woman. And you know what? It's GREAT. All of this internal monologue not only makes Jazz a fully-rounded character, it also helps to move the story along.

So care for your characters as you're writing your book. Even if, like Freddy Lounds in Thomas Harris' *Red Dragon*, they are doomed. When Freddy dies, even if your sympathy for him is limited because of his prior actions, it still hits like the death of a real person. The same for Eduard Delacroix in Stephen King's *Green Mile*. He's a raping, murdering bastard... yet still, when he experiences his "bad death", you feel for him. You still think, "No one should die like that". Why? Because he's real to you. Because Stephen King cared for him, you care for him.

STEP 7: WRAPPING IT ALL UP

Did a teacher ever write on a paper of yours something like "unsatisfactory conclusion"? I know that I saw that note more than once, especially in English Comp.

Now that you're ready to end your story, you definitely want a "satisfactory conclusion". And this doesn't necessarily mean a resounding ending. You can leave unanswered questions and unresolved storylines, as long as you meant to leave them unresolved. Keep in mind that your reader can tell if you did it on purpose or not. You don't want your reader, when talking to their friends about your story to mention an "unsatisfactory conclusion". So how do you avoid that?

Satisfying Conclusion

The conclusion of your story is the most important element for a reader to decide if they'll seek you out again or not, so you want an ending that will leave them fulfilled, but wanting more at some point. Discovering a new writer is a little like discovering a terrific new restaurant in that way. When your meal is done, you think, "Man, that was good! I can't wait to get hungry so that I can eat here again!"

Think of the books that you've read and movies that you've seen that have a great ending, whether it wraps everything up neatly or not. The narrator ridding himself of Tyler Durden in *Fight Club*. The one ring going in to the fires of Mount Doom in *The Return of the King*. Randall Flag and his community of ne'er do wells going up in a radioactive explosion in *The Stand*. Norman Bates awaiting his legal fate in *Psycho*.

The best way to create this type of ending is to make sure that you've got all of your T's crossed and your I's dotted by the end of the story. Make sure that you've wrapped up the story at hand for your protagonist. It's even possible to create a satisfying cliffhanger ending by introducing a new element on the last page, or the last paragraph, or even the last line of a story or last scene of a screenplay. Perhaps my favorite example of this is from the film *Eddie and the Cruisers*. The entire film is about a reporter's search for the mysterious sixties rock singer Eddie Wilson. She talks to former lovers, friends and band mates to try to find out about the mystery man who had disappeared twenty years before. In the final scene of the film, you see the documentary ending on a television set in a store window with a shot of Eddie Wilson as he appeared when he was a rock singer. When that fades out, you see the viewer's reflection in the window... and it is Eddie Wilson. Bearded, twenty years older, but clearly the man. In that one scene the director and screenwriter, Martin Davidson, basically undid every solution that the protagonist thought that she had discovered. And it was GREAT. The very definition of an "OMG" ending.

The best way to create an ending that will leave your reader frustrated, and may result in them throwing whatever contains your story at the cat, is to simply not end the story so that you may write a sequel. If you do this, no one will read it. A prime example of this is David Lynch's cult classic television show *Twin Peaks*. Throughout the entire first season, we get to know the odd inhabitants of *Twin Peaks* and how they relate to a murdered girl named Laura Palmer. We watched this mystery develop, anxiously awaiting the season finale. When the finale finally arrived, we discovered... nothing. According to Lynch, he NEVER wanted the murder of Laura Palmer resolved, and had apparently convinced the network that this was a good tactic. But when the second season premiered to anemic ratings that only got worse and worse as it progressed, they ultimately did decide to solve the mystery about halfway through the season. The problem is that because they didn't expect to solve it, they didn't have anything to follow it up.

Suspenseful Ending

There are two types of suspenseful ending: one that leaves the viewer satisfied due to a twist or some last-minute information, and one that leaves them frustrated because it seems to only exist to make a sequel or the next season possible.

The first type of ending is exemplified by the original *Friday the 13th* in 1980, or the original *Planet of the Apes* with Charlton Heston. In *Friday the 13th*, we learn, in what we think is the final moments of the film, that it was not the presumed drowned little boy, Jason Voorhees, that had been doing the killing, but his mother. That would have been immensely satisfying by itself, but then, as we see the protagonist floating on a boat on Crystal Lake, we see Jason himself rise from the depths to attack her. In the now-famous ending of *Planet of the Apes*, Heston discovers the remains of the Statue of Liberty, which tells him that he had been on his own Earth all along, and not on another planet as he had presumed.

The thing that makes these endings successful is the fact that, in both, we are given new information that changes the story to some degree.

Another way to create a good suspenseful ending is to put a coda on a film. These have come to be known as "teasers". Marvel Studios has brought these to a science with their superhero films, starting with the post-credit appearance of Samuel L. Jackson in *Iron Man* talking about the "Avengers Initiative". By presenting us with a teaser, Marvel is letting us know that, although that particular story is finished, there will be more from that character to follow. In the seventies and eighties, films would do this by putting a text tag at the end of the credits saying "(this character) will return in (this film). Of course, in some cases, such as *The Sword and the Sorcerer*, this never happened.

The unsatisfying suspenseful ending is exemplified by almost all the *Friday the 13th* series following the first one. You think that Jason is defeated? Oh, no... didn't you see his arm move?

These are endings that don't add anything to the story, and sometimes fly in the face of logic itself.

The Disney television series *Once Upon a Time* also fell into this trap. Just when you thought that the story was wrapped up, here comes a new evil queen who will be the villain in the next season. The season endings of *Smallville* that I mentioned earlier fall in to this category as well. After the first couple of seasons ended with all of the major characters in mortal peril, there was no more suspense because the viewer knew that it was all going to work out.

The easiest ways to avoid this trap are to know in advance how your story is going to turn out, making sure that all of the major story points in the story are wrapped up, and not going into the story thinking that you have the beginning of a franchise on your hands. Of course, the last stipulation is void if you launch the story as the first book in a series. If you let your reader know that they are in for a series, then they won't feel ripped off when they reach the end and the monster is still at large, or a new peril rises. You do this by titling your story with a story title and a series title and number. For example, Piers Anthony wrote a series of books called *The Incarnations of Immortality*, and his first book, *On A Pale Horse* was plainly titled *The Incarnations of Immortality, Book One.*

Going Out With A Bang

I love stories that go out with a bang. Movies that leave you breathless from the onslaught of story or action that come flying your way in the last scenes, or books that do so in the last chapters.

The most literal example of this is the movie *Fight Club*, as Edward Norton and Helena Bonham Carter stand in an empty upper floor of an office building watching buildings around them explode. An example from horror cinema would either be the 1933 or 2005 versions of *King Kong*. From the time that Kong escapes in New York until he falls from the Empire State Building, they are both almost entirely non-stop action and suspense. Will Faye Wray or Naomi Watts fall to their death? Will the airplanes defeat Kong? You just don't know until they happen.

Edgar Allan Poe may have begun the trend of ending horror stories with a bang with his *Fall of the House of Usher*, with the literal fall of the house of Usher. When the building collapses, the story is breathtakingly over with a breath-taking finale. Stephen King manages the "with a bang" ending in many of his books, including *It*, *The Tommyknockers*, and the greatly underappreciated *Needful Things*. In each of these stories, the action is drawn through the book to a crescendo in the last chapter.

When you are planning on ending your story with a bang, however, you should very clearly have that ending in mind when you begin, so that you're not just setting off proverbial fireworks. Remember Chekhov's rifle in the first chapter? All of the fireworks that you set off should have some significance for your characters, and for the story itself. If it doesn't serve the story, it should be chucked overboard.

So, for example, if you're planning on destroying the town that the story was set in, as King did in *Needful Things*, there should be indications throughout the story that there's simply no other way that the story can end. In King's first published novel, *Carrie*, you routinely see Carrietta White with her crazy zealot of a mother suffer humiliation at the hands of her classmates and the townsfolk, as well as get tantalizing hints of the power that lives within her until you know that there is no way for the story to end other than spectacular tragedy.

If you don't do that, if you don't at least hint in your story that the literary train that you're riding is doomed to crash, then when the crash does come, it's empty. It becomes, as Shakespeare said, "A tale full of sound and fury, told by an idiot, signifying nothing."

CONCLUSION

So you have a story that you want to tell. I hope that I have given your some clues that will help you tell that story in a satisfactory manner. A manner which will cause your readers to come to you, slap you on the back, and tell you what a great job you did telling the story.

Stephen King tells a story about opening his mail one day to find that a reader had mailed him a paperback copy of *'Salem's Lot*, along with a note saying, "I couldn't finish reading this... it scared the hell out of me." King wrote a note back to the reader that said, "Good, that's what it's supposed to do" and sent the book back to her. Emulating Stephen King in this way, in the way of being determined to tell a story that will give a reader chills and keep them turning the pages until the very end is a good thing. Personally, I spent a weekend reading the last hundred pages of *Needful Things* because I simply could not stop reading until I saw how it all worked out. Emulating King by being determined to become rich off your stories is not a good thing. Not only will it cause you to tell your story in a way that doesn't necessarily serve the story, but is only designed to appeal to the widest number of people, which is usually the lowest common denominator.

I read an article recently about how horror films have become much more thoughtful, requiring more from the reader than slasher films or body horror films. The author of the article pointed out that, on the movie review aggregation website Rotten Tomatoes, "think piece" horror films inevitably got high ratings from critics and low ratings from viewers. Body horror films and slasher films were the opposite. There is a best-selling author who came on the scene in the late twentieth century who simply can't write. His syntax is bad. He breaks the cardinal rule of "show, don't tell" by overusing –ly adverbs, especially the adverb "quietly" in one of his books. The characters in this book nod quietly, wave quietly, smile quietly, and throughout all of this, I kept wondering how you do those things in any other way. That author, like King, is rich. But his riches come from presenting an idea that American audiences hadn't been exposed to in wide numbers (that he lifted from another book that did not sell so well because it was marketed as non-fiction) instead of telling a compelling story.

So please, tell a good story well, and be satisfying with being a toiler in the mines of fiction instead of telling a bad story poorly in the hopes that the masses will latch onto it and make you rich.

Thank you again for taking this journey with me. If you have enjoyed the book, please go to the website where you purchased it and leave a review so that others may enjoy it.

Thanks! Happy writing!

Randal Schaffer (contributing author for HowExpert.com)

About the Expert

Randal Schaffer's tastes were turned in the direction of horror with the first film that he saw at the age of four, *The Pit and the Pendulum* with Vincent Price. The first story that he "wrote" using comic-strip style panels was about a mad scientist who creates a giant moth-man who then bit his head off. As an early reader, Randal began devouring H. P. Lovecraft and E. A. Poe in grade school, moving on to Stephen King and Clive Barker. He is writing his own series called "Shivers: Tales of Erotic Nightmare". The first of these, *Going All the Way* is currently on Amazon, to be followed soon by book 2, *Lady Frankenstein's Lover*.

HowExpert publishes quick 'how to' guides on all topics from A to Z by everyday experts. Visit HowExpert.com to learn more.

Recommended Resources

- HowExpert.com – Quick 'How To' Guides on All Topics from A to Z by Everyday Experts.
- HowExpert.com/free – Free HowExpert Email Newsletter.
- HowExpert.com/books – HowExpert Books
- HowExpert.com/courses – HowExpert Courses
- HowExpert.com/membership – HowExpert Membership Site
- HowExpert.com/writers – Write About Your #1 Passion/Knowledge/Expertise & Become a HowExpert Author.
- HowExpert.com/resources – Additional HowExpert Recommended Resources
- YouTube.com/HowExpert – Subscribe to HowExpert YouTube.
- Instagram.com/HowExpert – Follow HowExpert on Instagram.
- Facebook.com/HowExpert – Follow HowExpert on Facebook.

CPSIA information can be obtained
at www.ICGtesting.com
Printed in the USA
LVHW020037121122
732945LV00003B/73

9 781647 580568